DO YOU ENJOY B̶█████████?

WOULD YOU █████████
NIGHTMARES
INSTEAD OF SWEET DREAMS?

ARE YOU HAPPY ONLY WHEN
SHAKING WITH FEAR?

CONGRATULATIONS ! ! ! !

YOU'VE MADE A WISE CHOICE.

THIS BOOK IS THE DOORWAY
TO ALL THAT MAY FRIGHTEN YOU.

GET READY FOR

COLD, CLAMMY SHIVERS
RUNNING UP AND DOWN YOUR SPINE!

NOW, OPEN THE DOOR–
IF YOU DARE !!!!

Shivers

THE HAUNTING HOUSE

M. D. Spenser

Paradise Press, Inc.

Plantation, Florida

Published by Paradise Press, Inc. by arrangement with River Publishing, Inc. All right, title and interest to the "SHIVERS" logo and design are owned by River Publishing, Inc. No portion of the "SHIVERS" logo and design may be reproduced in part or whole without prior written permission from River Publishing, Inc. An application for a registered trademark of the "SHIVERS" logo and design is pending with the Federal Patent and Trademark office.

ISBN 1-57657-051-7

EXCLUSIVE DISTRIBUTION BY PARADISE PRESS, INC.

Cover Design by George Paturzo
Cover Illustration by Eddie Roseboom

Printed in the U.S.A.

To Jiři

THE
HAUNTING
HOUSE

Chapter One

Caitlin was afraid.

After all, moving to a new house is never easy.

Moving means saying good-bye to old friends. Moving means going to a new school where everyone is unfamiliar. Moving means settling into a strange home in a strange city when you liked the old home and the old city just fine.

Caitlin had never moved before and it did not sound like fun to her. So what if her father had a new job as a scientist in the next city over? Why couldn't he just drive a little further to work every day?

At least she wouldn't have to share a bedroom anymore with her dorky younger sister, Lynne! That was one good thing about the move.

Each girl now would have her own bedroom, with a bathroom attached.

To Caitlin, Lynne was a big pain in the neck.

Lynne was only nine years old and didn't know nearly as much about anything as Caitlin, who was almost thirteen.

But Lynne liked to pretend she was just as smart. That annoyed Caitlin.

Actually, Caitlin did not mind that as much as she minded the way Lynne always caused trouble. Lynne liked getting into everything she was not supposed to get into. And she always managed to blame Caitlin when things went wrong.

Caitlin ended up in trouble for things she hadn't done. It just wasn't fair!

But in the new home, Caitlin could lock the door to her big bedroom and be all by herself.

As her father drove the family toward their new home thirty miles away, Caitlin smiled when she thought about having a private bedroom and bathroom for the first time in her life.

Maybe her parents would even let her have her own phone! And her own TV and her own computer!

Well . . . maybe not.

Caitlin decided she had better wait a while to ask for anything new. She knew her parents were spending a lot of money to repair the old house they had just bought in the suburbs outside Detroit.

They had always wanted to buy a home that was almost a hundred years old, like this one, and then fix it up. It was an abandoned house on the end of a dark dirt road, far from the busy center of the city.

No one had lived in the house for ten years! And the people who lived there last had left in a hurry — without even selling the place.

That seemed very weird to Caitlin.

She had only seen the house once and it looked like a creaky old dump to her. But her parents thought the place was "cool" — that was the exact word they had used.

Caitlin just rolled her eyes when they said this.

Why did parents always try to use words like that, anyway?

Besides, what could be cool about this house? It looked like something out of an old black-and-white horror movie!

She was sure the place was haunted or something.

Caitlin didn't get scared easily, like some kids.

And she didn't really believe in ghosts, even though she had a book about them.

But everything about the house seemed frightening to her.

It was a large two-story wooden house with wide, white shutters beside every window and a huge, dark basement. The home had old thick-paned windows and old wood floors and old heavy doors in every room. And it was topped with a steep old roof with some of the shingles missing.

When you walked around inside, the house looked old and smelled old. And it sounded old as you stepped across the floorboards. They groaned.

The broad lawn around the house was surrounded by woods, though the trees had no leaves at this time of year. It was already past Thanksgiving, nearly winter.

Caitlin thought the trees looked exactly like an attacking army of stick people, with long, sharp claws on the end of their limbs, ready to tear apart anything that got in their way.

Maybe the army of trees was the reason the last family had left the house so quickly. Maybe the

4

trees had tried to kill everyone who lived there. Maybe the tree-claws had strangled someone in the middle of the night.

Caitlin laughed under her breath in the car, and told herself not to believe such silly things. Things that don't move can't attack people, she thought. Trees couldn't hurt anyone.

They were planted in the ground as firmly as the house. And everyone knew that a house could never do anything to hurt someone!

But, for some reason she could not put her finger on, Caitlin felt like something bad was going to happen at the new house.

She did not know what exactly. And she hoped she was wrong.

Now, out of the woods, the house loomed up in front of them. Their father pulled into the driveway. Caitlin and Lynne shoved each other to get out of the car first.

"Last one to the back yard has to do the dishes tonight!" Lynne yelled, pushing out the door ahead of her sister.

"No way!" Caitlin shouted.

"Way!" Lynne bellowed, running toward the back yard.

"You kids be very careful out back!" their father hollered. "And stay away from the hole!"

Behind the house, a wide hole gaped in the middle of the lawn. Just a big, empty hole in the ground. No one knew why it was there.

Caitlin's parents said the old owners must have been building a swimming pool when they'd had to move out in a hurry. Caitlin's father had said he might finish building the pool in the springtime.

Caitlin and Lynne thought having their own swimming pool would be excellent! Maybe the new house would not be so bad after it was all fixed up, Caitlin thought as she chased her sister to the back yard.

"Beat ya! Beat ya!" Lynne yelled. "You do dishes tonight!"

"No *way!*" Caitlin answered firmly. "I didn't agree we were racing! Besides you cheated to get a head start. You're such a little kid!"

"Am *not!* I'm almost as tall as you are!" Lynne said, pouting like a little kid.

The two sisters walked around the back lawn for a few minutes, looking at the shrubs outside the house and the trees at the edge of the brown grass.

Suddenly, Lynne was gone!

"Lynne! Lynne!" Caitlin called. *"Lynne! Where are you?"*

Caitlin looked around — toward the woods, toward the house, toward the hole. Everywhere!

Lynne was nowhere in sight.

"Lynne! This isn't funny!" Caitlin cried. She was becoming frantic. *"Lynne,* where *are* you?"

She saw no sign of her sister. And she heard no sound except the rattling and clacking of tree limbs in the cold autumn winds.

What was going on here? Caitlin wondered desperately. How could anything have gone wrong so fast?

Her family had only been at the new house ten minutes and something bad already had happened.

Something very bad!

Something much worse than she had ever imagined!

Her younger sister, Lynne, had simply disappeared — vanished from the back yard without a trace!

Chapter Two

Where had Lynne gone?

What could have happened to her? Was she dead?

Maybe the trees really *had* attacked somehow, grabbing Lynne in their claws and passing her from limb to limb until she was deep in the woods.

Caitlin felt terrible about all the mean things she had ever said to her sister. She promised herself that she would never utter another nasty word to her — if only something could bring her dear sister back!

"Lynne, oh no! *Oh no, oh no, oh no,*" Caitlin repeated again and again.

Then she felt a small stone hit her in the back!

Caitlin turned — and ducked as another small stone arched slowly toward her.

"Lynne!" Caitlin said angrily. "I'm going to kill you!"

She could hear giggling. Now, she understood what was happening.

She walked over to the edge of the hole in the ground and looked down.

Lynne was hiding inside the hole, tossing pebbles at her sister.

"You think you're funny!" Caitlin snapped. "This isn't funny at all, Lynne! I thought you were hurt or something had happened to you! Next time, you might be hurt and I won't come looking for you! That's not smart!"

"Oh yes it is! Smarter than you are! It fooled *you*," Lynne crowed.

Lynne really did act much younger than her sister, you see. She had not yet learned that it's always a mistake to pretend that something is the matter when everything is really OK.

Even though Lynne was only nine, she looked older. She was tall and slim, with pretty brown hair that fell over her shoulders. She had large, round eyes and even, white teeth and a beautiful smile.

Caitlin was not as pretty as her sister. But it didn't matter.

Not to Lynne. Not to their mother. Not to their father.

Not even to Caitlin herself.

Everyone in the family understood that what's inside a person means more than the way someone looks. They all knew that it's much more important to be smart and kind and considerate and loving than it is to look pretty.

"There's nothing wrong with looking beautiful, of course," their father told them. "As long as you understand you can't judge someone by beauty alone."

Caitlin was short for her age, and a little heavy. She wore braces to straighten her crooked teeth. Her hair was blond but on the stringy side, and cut close to her head. She had to wear contact lenses so she could see clearly.

Both sisters were very bright — even if Lynne still had some lessons to learn about staying out of trouble. And both had been popular in their old school.

Lynne was something of a tomboy who liked to hang out with the guys her age, playing baseball and football. She was strong and athletic.

Not Caitlin. She was a talented musician who performed on both the piano and the guitar during school concerts. And she loved to sit around the house, even when it was sunny and warm outside, reading novels and poetry or talking with good friends on the phone.

Of course, Caitlin was by far the more mature of the two. And she tried to play the protective big sister now.

"Lynne, get out of that hole right away!" she said. "It's dangerous in there! And if Dad catches you, you'll be in trouble."

"Nah, nah-nah, nah-nah, nah!" Lynne taunted. She loved to drive her sister crazy. "I'm staying in here as long as I want. And you can't *make* me get out if I don't want to!"

"Listen, Lynne, if you don't get out of there right now, I'm going to go tell Dad," Caitlin said.

"Go ahead! Tattletale!" Lynne said. She knew Caitlin almost never tattled to their parents about anything she did.

"OK, I'm coming down there to get you!" Caitlin said. "It's not safe down there!"

As her sister giggled mischievously, Caitlin knelt down at the side of the great hole and lowered herself in.

She grabbed her sister by the coat and started pulling her toward the edge of the hole. Lynne laughed and half-tried to get away.

"Come on, get out!" Caitlin shouted. "Right now, Lynne!"

"Uh-uh, no way!" Lynne teased, struggling to get free. "I didn't want to move here anyway. I hate this house! I'm going to live in this hole!"

The two sisters wrestled and grabbed at each other in the hole, with Lynne laughing and Caitlin getting angry.

Neither one noticed the danger right over their heads.

Directly above them was a monstrous pile of dirt and sand and rocks, everything that had been dug from the ground to make the hole. It was packed into one enormous mound, where the earth and stone had rested undisturbed beside the edge of the hole for a decade.

Until now.

As Caitlin and Lynne wrestled, a few grains of sand spilled from the top of the pile into the hole. They dropped right next to the girls' feet.

But they didn't notice.

Several more grains of sand and dirt, along with a few pebbles, dribbled down beside the girls. Still, Caitlin and Lynne saw nothing.

"I hate this house! I'm going to stay right in this hole," Lynne repeated, laughing.

And then dozens and dozens of grains of dirt and sand spilled into the pit, along with clumps of clay and rock. Some of the sand fell into Lynne's hair and across Caitlin's shoulder.

The girls stopped wrestling and looked up — and were horrified by what they saw.

The entire mass of dirt and rock was quivering, teetering on the edge of the great hole. The mound was starting to crumble, right over their heads!

"Aaaaaaaaaaaaaahhhhhhhhh!" Lynne screamed.

"Avalanche!" Caitlin shouted.

This old house is going to kill my sister and me, Caitlin thought, in a panic. We're going to be buried alive! There is nothing we can do to get away!

Slowly at first, and then faster and faster, the pile of earth and stones started to tumble into the hole on top of them.

Chapter Three

Caitlin was sure it was too late!

The mass of dirt and rocks began to topple over like a stack of cans someone had bumped into in the supermarket. Everything rained into the hole at once. Enough soil and stones to bury two girls.

Both girls screamed in fright.

Lynne leapt desperately to one side, away from the falling pile of earth. As she jumped, she grabbed Caitlin by the neck and pulled hard.

The girls tumbled across the hole, just out of the way of the collapsing dirt.

They looked back to see a cloud of dust rise into the air from the fallen mountain of soil.

"Wow, that was close!" Lynne said, breathing heavily from fear.

"I thought we were going to die for sure,"

Caitlin said, her voice quivering. She could feel her whole body shaking. "I've never seen so much dirt fall in one place. It was awful! But you saved us, Lynne! If you hadn't pulled me away, we'd be buried under all that dirt right now! We were really lucky!"

But then the parents of these two lucky girls came racing around the corner. And the parents' faces looked very afraid.

"Lynne! Caitlin!" their father called. "Girls! Are you all right?"

"Girls! Girls!" their mother cried. "What happened? What happened? Are you safe?"

"Hi, we're down here," Caitlin said sheepishly. "Uh, we had a little accident."

"Hi, Mom!" Lynne said, as if nothing had happened. "No biggie. We're OK. Just some dirt fell into the hole. No problem."

"No problem? Do you know what could have happened if all that dirt fell on top of you?" their father said angrily. "Look at you two! You're a mess. Now get out of there! I told you to stay away from the hole!"

"But, Dad . . . " Caitlin started to say, trying to

explain.

"Don't you 'but Dad' me, young lady! You're old enough to know better than to play near some place that's so dangerous," her father interrupted. "You should have made sure neither of you were even near that hole!"

He helped pull his two daughters out of the pit. Caitlin's pants were smeared with mud. The sleeve of Lynne's jacket was torn.

"But, Dad, I didn't . . . " Caitlin began to explain again. But it was no use.

"Now, I don't want to hear any excuses," their father said. "You both could have been killed! I want you two to go inside and stay there the rest of the day. And I want you to stay away from this hole from now on! Do you understand me this time?"

"Yes, sir," Caitlin said quietly, looking down.

"Yes, sir," Lynne said, fidgeting with her torn jacket.

The sisters walked slowly toward the house. Caitlin was getting angry.

Lynne had done it again, she thought. Her sister had gotten her in trouble — and Lynne was the one who had disobeyed and gone into the hole.

It just wasn't fair!

But she had to admit, her sister *had* saved her life! She couldn't get too mad at her this time.

"You wouldn't listen to me when I said it was dangerous in that hole!" she said to Lynne. "You're such a little kid!"

When the girls got inside, each went into her own bathroom and took a long, hot shower, washing the dirt from her face and hands and hair. Then each started unpacking the boxes filled with her belongings.

Moving is such a pain, Caitlin thought. Already she missed her old house and her old city and her old friends.

This new place is so weird, she thought.

Something about the house just did not seem right. For reasons she could not explain, she simply did not like it.

She decided that maybe she should walk around and take a better look at everything. Her parents were working outside, trying to fix some of the things that were cracked or broken. And there were many.

Maybe her home would not seem so weird once she got to know all the old rooms and hallways better.

So she went exploring.

From one dark room to another, Caitlin wandered.

Down the narrow hallways, opening the heavy, moaning doors that sealed off each room in the house. But somehow, in every room she entered, she felt like an intruder.

It was as if she were an unwelcome stranger, disturbing the peace of the silent old home.

First, she opened the door to the dining room.

Mmmmmwwwwaaaaaaahhhhhnnnn!

There was nothing there, except the dining room furniture and boxes the movers had brought from their old house.

And the odd feeling of being watched by unfriendly walls.

Then, she opened the thick door to her father's study.

Kkkkkrrrraaaaaaaaggggg!

Nothing there either, except more furniture

20

and more boxes. And more sensations of being observed — even though no one was around.

And then, she opened the door to the living room.

Wwwwwwwwwooooorrrrrr!

Nothing but the sofas and chairs and tables. And the same strange feelings.

And some footprints . . .

Footprints!

These were like no other footprints Caitlin ever had seen. They were very large prints, left in the thin layer of dust that coated the floor.

They were the footprints of a big man. A *very* big man!

The man who made these footprints would have to be at least seven feet tall, Caitlin figured. And if he was seven feet tall, he probably would weigh three hundred pounds!

Caitlin knew that her father was nowhere near seven feet tall or three hundred pounds. And none of the movers was that large, either.

Someone else was in the house!

Maybe this was why she felt as if somebody

was watching her every move. Maybe somebody was!

Some massive man was hiding in their home, skulking from room to room.

Watching.

Waiting.

Plotting and planning.

He could be a robber. He could be a kidnapper.

He could be a killer!

Whatever he was, he was up to no good.

Caitlin felt she had to find out what it was. She did not want her father to surprise the man and get hurt.

She decided to track the footprints through the dust by herself. She planned to sneak up on the man without letting him spot her.

Then she would tell her father where the man was hidden, and her father could call the police!

But for now, she had to be quiet! *Very* quiet!

She had to follow the dusty footprints of a very large, very bad man.

And she had to pray that he wouldn't find her before she found him!

Chapter Four

The footprints of the monster man trailed off through the living room, circled around the main sofa, and headed into the back hallway.

Filled with dread, Caitlin tiptoed down the hall, following the path.

At any moment, the enormous, powerful *thing* might reach out and grab her!

Trying to be as brave as possible, Caitlin bent low to the floor, looking at the faint prints in the dust.

They led down the narrow dark hallway — directly into the kitchen.

A thick, creaky door separated the kitchen from the hall. Caitlin stood in the shadows, holding her breath, trying to get up enough nerve to push it open.

"Don't chicken out now," she told herself. "You have to do this to help Dad!"

After a few deep breaths — in and out and in and out — she started a countdown to make herself look inside the kitchen.

"Ready?" she asked herself. "OK. One, two, three. . . .Go!"

Gently, inch by inch, she pushed the door open. Little by little, she could see more of the kitchen. And then more. And then more.

She saw no monster man.

But he might be hiding right behind the door, waiting to grab her arm when she reached in far enough. Or he might be tucked inside the kitchen closet, ready to pounce if she walked inside.

Desperately, Caitlin tried to be even quieter, hoping to make absolutely no sound at all.

Then it happened: The door squeaked.

Cccccrrrrrrraaaawwwwwwmm!

Caitlin wanted to turn and run. The monster man was probably reaching around the door to grab her by the throat.

Before she could flee, she heard a familiar voice.

"What are you doing, dipbrain?" said Lynne,

with a laugh. "Why are you sneaking around the kitchen?"

"Ohhhhh, nooooo!" Caitlin groaned.

Now she understood what had been happening.

Lynne was sitting on a kitchen chair, happily munching on a peanut butter-and-jelly sandwich. Her feet were resting on top of the kitchen table.

And on her feet were huge, fuzzy pink slippers.

Slippers the size of a monster man's feet!

Lynne was smiling. Caitlin was not.

"It was *you!*" Caitlin said. "I should have known! It's *always* you!"

"What are you talking about, Caitlin? I didn't do anything this time," Lynne answered, biting into her sandwich again.

"You do something wrong even when you're not trying to do something wrong," Caitlin snapped. "Where did you get those slippers? I've never seen them before!"

"Mom bought them for me when she took me to that dollar store at the mall last week," Lynne said. "This is the first time I've worn them. So what? What *about* my slippers?"

"Oh, never mind! Why should I even bother explaining anything to you? You wouldn't understand anyway," Caitlin replied. "Just leave me alone. I don't know why I take anything seriously around this family. I should just understand that when anything goes wrong, you're always the reason."

Lynne got up from her chair and slid her pink slippers along the tile floor, as if she were ice skating. She skated over to the kitchen cabinets and opened a drawer to get out a knife.

"I'm still hungry. I think I'm going to make another sandwich," she said. "Do you want one? I'll make it for you — though I don't know why I should be nice to *you!* You always say such mean things to me. I think you're even worse since we moved. I don't like living in this house at all!"

"Why do you have to be such a kid all the time? Can't you grow up?" Caitlin asked. "No, I don't want a sandwich. I'm going up to my room to unpack. Just don't come in my room! You're such a jerk!"

Caitlin turned to walk out of the kitchen. A sudden scream stopped her.

"Oooooooooowwwww!" Lynne hollered. "My finger!"

Caitlin turned angrily.

"Stop playing stupid games, Lynne!" Caitlin said. "I told you before, it's not smart!"

"My finger! Oooowwww!" Lynne whimpered. "The drawer closed on it. I'm hurt, Caitlin."

"Yeah, right," Caitlin said. "Good try! But I'm not falling for any more of your stupid pranks!"

"It's not a prank!" Lynne said, a tear running down her right cheek. "It *hurt!* The drawer just closed on my finger. Come here and see for yourself."

Caitlin walked over and examined her sister's finger. It *was* hurt — already swollen and bruised.

"How could you possibly have done that?" Caitlin asked.

"*I* didn't do it! That's what I'm trying to tell you," Lynne whined. "The *drawer* did it! All by itself, Caitlin. It closed on my finger without me touching it! As if it *wanted* to catch my finger in there. As if the drawer was trying to hurt me real bad!"

Chapter Five

"That's just silly!" Caitlin said. "Drawers don't move all by themselves!"

But in her heart, she was not so sure.

This was a strange house. Somehow, she realized that right away.

Maybe the house was even stranger than she had imagined.

"Tell me what happened, right now," she said firmly. "I don't want to play around with your kids' games anymore. You must have bumped the drawer somehow, Lynne."

"Honest! I'm telling you the truth, Caitlin," Lynne answered. "I just reached in the drawer for a knife. And the drawer started to slam shut on my fingers — fast! I tried to pull my hand out in time but the drawer caught my finger really hard."

The proof that Lynne wasn't lying about the injury was right there — in one very black-and-blue finger. And her voice sounded as if she was not lying about anything else, either.

Still, this was too much to believe. Drawers could not move without someone touching them.

Could they?

And even if it was true, what could she do about it? What could anyone do about it?

There was no use telling her parents — they would *never* believe a ridiculous story like that. No one would.

So Caitlin tried to pretend nothing was wrong. She told Lynne that she must have bumped the drawer somehow, maybe with an arm or a hip.

And she told herself the same thing. As she walked up the stairs alone to her room, she tried hard to make herself believe it. Lynne had bumped the drawer into her own finger. That was all that had happened.

Nothing was wrong with her family's new house. Nothing whatsoever.

But, deep inside herself, Caitlin knew the truth was something else. Something too frightening to even think about.

Chapter Six

Caitlin was surprised when she got back upstairs. Surprised — and troubled.

The door to her room was wide open.

"That's strange," she said to herself. "I *know* I closed that door! And Lynne was downstairs. And Mom and Dad are still outside working. Hmmmm."

But she shrugged her shoulders and shook her head and again pretended to herself that nothing was wrong. Doors don't open by themselves, she thought.

And she tried hard to believe it.

Until she noticed that her window was open, too. Even though it was almost winter outside and the cold late-autumn air was filling her room.

She *knew* no one in her family would have opened the window, wasting expensive heat.

But if not her family, then who *had* opened it?

Then Caitlin saw that clothes she had unpacked from three boxes and hung up in her closet also had been moved.

But moved in a very strange way.

The clothes were all back in the boxes, which were neatly sealed with heavy packing tape.

Caitlin shuddered with fear.

"How could this possibly happen?" she asked. "My door is left open. The window is letting in cold air. And my boxes are packed up again! It's just not possible!"

Then Caitlin snapped her fingers, realizing what must have happened. Her expression changed from fear to irritation.

"Lynne!" she said out loud.

It *had* to be Lynne, pulling some stunt again. It was *always* Lynne.

So Caitlin marched downstairs toward the kitchen to scold her little sister. But when she reached the bottom of the stairs, Lynne was already there, looking at her with puzzled eyes.

"Hey, Cait, why is it so cold in here?" Lynne asked. "Did you turn down the heat?"

"*You* should know! You left my window wide open with the freezing air coming inside," Caitlin snapped.

"Huh? You're crazy. I didn't open your window. I haven't been in your room once since we got here," Lynne said.

"Don't lie to me, Lynne! It had to be you," Caitlin said.

"I'm *not* lying, Cait! Why don't you ever believe me? I have not been in your room. I *swear*!" Lynne said.

She sure sounded as if she was telling the truth.

Caitlin did not know what to believe. Then she noticed the goose bumps on her arms.

"You know, you're right about something. It *is* cold in this house. Too cold to be caused by just one open window," she said, scratching her head. "I turned the heat up when we came inside. It should be nice and warm in here. But it seems to be getting colder instead of warmer."

She walked over to the thermostat and found something very peculiar.

The heat was turned off.

Not just turned down, but completely off. As if there were not a house full of people that needed heat.

As if no one were going to live in the house at all.

Who would turn off the heat when it was so cold and windy outside?

Lynne would never do that, even if she had been playing some stupid kid's trick in Caitlin's room. Lynne complained more than anybody else in the family about feeling cold. She always wanted the heat turned up high whenever it was the least bit chilly.

And her parents certainly would not turn off the heat. And Caitlin knew she hadn't done it.

But someone had. Or some*thing* had!

"Lynne, this just weirds me out!" Caitlin said, trying to hide her fears from her little sister. "Very strange things are happening in this house. I can't explain any of them. You *swear* you haven't been in my room? You're not fooling around with me? This is serious, Lynne!"

"No, honest, Cait. I swear!" Lynne said emphatically.

"Then this really is very, very weird, Lynne. The drawer, the door, the window, the heat," Caitlin said, thinking about everything that had happened. "And my clothes! That was the most bizarre thing of all! How could they have been packed back in their boxes?"

"Huh? What door? What clothes? What do you mean they were packed back in their boxes?" Lynne asked.

"Never mind, Lynne. I'll tell you everything later. But we have to decide how to break this to Mom and Dad. We have to find some way to make them believe what's happening here," Caitlin said quickly. "Our lives might be in danger!"

She paused to think again.

"What do you mean, Cait? What *is* happening in our new house? How are we in so much danger?" Lynne said.

Her voice sounded very worried.

"There is only one explanation, Lynne," Caitlin explained. "There's only one answer for all the weird things that are going on everywhere around here. I always knew something was strange about this place.

But now I know what it is — for sure!"

But even though the answer was in her mind, Caitlin was afraid to say it. Afraid that if she spoke the words, that would make them come true.

"What? What? What do you *mean?*" Lynne asked, almost frantic.

"It's the worst thing that could happen. Nothing worse can ever happen to a house! Our new home is haunted, Lynne," Caitlin said, reluctantly.

"The whole place is filled with ghosts!"

Chapter Seven

"*Ghosts?* You're *crazy*, Caitlin!" Lynne exclaimed. "I'm only nine years old and even I know there's no such thing as ghosts!"

"Oh, yeah? I didn't believe in them either. But come with me and I'll prove it to you," Caitlin answered, in that know-it-all voice girls sometimes use with younger sisters.

Caitlin turned the heat back on and walked upstairs with Lynne, explaining about the opened door and the opened window and the clothes packed back in their boxes.

"I can *feel* something in this house, Lynne. I just know it. I've always known it, since the first moment I set foot in this place," Caitlin said, opening the door to her room. "There's a bad presence, like something or someone doesn't want us here. Come over to my desk and I'll show you what I mean about ghosts."

Caitlin pulled out one of the books she had unpacked from a moving company box earlier that day — a book all about the supernatural. It was called, *Ghosts, Goblins and Ghouls: The Real Story Behind House Hauntings.*

"When we were downstairs talking about everything that happened in our house, I remembered reading this book a couple years ago," Caitlin said, thumbing through the pages. "And that's when I knew for sure we had ghosts in our house. I'll show you, as soon as I find this one chapter about — Yeah, here it is."

She began to read to her frightened little sister from the ghost book. As she read, she became frightened, too:

"Ghosts are the spirits of people who died with some terrible conflict unresolved, or in some terrible pain. Often they died violently, by murder or suicide," the chapter about ghosts began.

"They can inhabit any building but especially are fond of older structures. Commonly, ghosts are

discovered haunting abandoned buildings such as houses, businesses and railroad stations. They create disturbances in the environment and can cause fear and misery — but never injury or death — for any living person who enters their habitat."

"Just because we live in an old abandoned house doesn't mean we have ghosts, you big jerk," Lynne said. "That stuff in the book doesn't mean anything."

"Let me finish reading this page to you, Lynne," Caitlin said. "I'm just getting to the part that proves we have ghosts."

She continued to read:

"Ghosts are looking for some way to resolve the pain or conflict that caused them to remain among the living after their bodies died. Sometimes these spirits do this through terrorizing human beings they come in contact with. Poltergeists are the most common form of terror employed by ghosts: Objects move around on their own. Doors, cabinets and drawers may open and close. Windows may shut so tight no one can pry them loose or open so far no one can close them again. Household items like furniture *and clothing sometimes disappear from one place, turning up somewhere unexpected.*"

"You see what I mean," Caitlin said nervously. "It sounds almost exactly like what happened to us. We have ghosts — and they're creating a poltergeist. We're living in a haunted house, Lynne!"

"But Cait, remember what the book said about ghosts not hurting people?" Lynne recalled. "It said ghosts 'can cause misery — but never injury or death — for any living person.' I was injured by that drawer. Look at how swollen and sore my finger is."

Lynne's index finger looked like a long blue thumb now, thick and bruised from being slammed in the drawer.

"It *can't* be ghosts, Caitlin. Whatever it is in the house, it hurt my finger pretty bad," Lynne said.

"Maybe the book is wrong about ghosts not ever injuring people. Or maybe we've got a really mean ghost!" Caitlin said. "There's just no other explanation. Our home is haunted, Lynne. We might as well face it and get Mom and Dad to believe it, too. And then they'll sell this house so we can move away!"

40

"But there was something else that happened to us, Cait. Remember how we almost got buried under all that dirt in the hole out back?" Lynne said. "Maybe that wasn't an accident, like we thought it was. Maybe something was trying to *murder* us!"

This made Caitlin stop to think. The huge mound of dirt certainly had fallen into the pit, nearly killing them both. And the drawer had seemed to close by itself right onto Lynne's finger, Caitlin had to admit.

But if not ghosts — what? What could be causing so much weirdness in one old home?

And, whatever it was, why was it trying to hurt her family?

This house was a terrible place to live!

Just then, the girls heard a tremendous crash and clatter, as if pieces of metal had splattered across the tile floor downstairs. The sound made both of them jump.

"Wha — uh, what was that?" Lynne asked, dreading the answer. "Was — uh, was it, uh — *ghosts*, do you think?"

"It sounded like something fell in the kitchen.

Probably the ghosts knocked something over to scare us again," Caitlin said. "Let's go see what happened."

Caitlin actually felt relieved as she hurried down the staircase with her sister. Now she was really sure there was at least one ghost, maybe more.

It seemed a lot better to imagine their house was haunted by a ghost that meant no harm, rather than by something else that really wanted to hurt people.

Probably the ghost had not wanted to catch Lynne's finger in the drawer. And probably the ghost had never really intended to bury the two sisters under the pile of dirt.

Ghosts were spooky but they were harmless. The book said so!

Lynne and Caitlin pushed open the squeaky kitchen door and found the silverware drawer on the floor, with knives and forks and spoons scattered everywhere. It was the same drawer that had closed so hard on Lynne's finger.

Then the girls heard another noise — like water running somewhere behind them.

They whirled around and saw their father at

the kitchen sink, behind the door. He was washing his hands.

"Dad, what happened here?" Caitlin asked. "Were you in the kitchen when the drawer came out? Did it just fly out of the cabinet on to the floor, or what?"

"Fly out? What the heck are you talking about, Caitlin?" their father said. "I cut myself on a knife when I reached into the drawer. And when I pulled my hand away quickly, this stupid old drawer came out and dropped on the floor."

"So *you* did this? You mean, the drawer just fell out by accident?" Caitlin asked, even more relieved now.

Maybe there wasn't a ghost or anything else in the house, after all. Not even one.

"How else would it fall out? As I said, I reached in the drawer and cut myself on a knife," the father said, wrapping a paper towel around his bleeding finger. "But one thing does seem kind of strange, I guess. Because I don't know exactly *how* I got cut. I hadn't even really touched the knife when I felt it slice through my skin."

"You hadn't touched it?" Lynne asked, looking uncomfortably at her sister.

"No, I really was only starting to reach in for the knife," their father replied, his eyebrows twisted in confusion. "It was almost like the knife jumped right out at my finger. I know that sounds silly but it all happened really fast. It just seemed like the knife came out of the drawer after me — as if it was trying to cut my finger right off!"

Chapter Eight

Caitlin and Lynne were startled.

"Dad, are you sure the knife jumped out at your finger?" Caitlin asked. Her voice wavered with tension. "Maybe it was just your imagination, huh?"

"Yeah, maybe everything happened so fast you really just cut yourself before you knew it," Lynne said.

The father looked at his daughters with a bewildered expression, then smiled.

"Listen, don't let your imaginations run wild, girls," he said. "Of *course* I cut myself on the knife. What else do you think happened? Knives don't jump out and cut people. I was only saying that's what it *seemed* like. It's great to have a vivid imagination — but don't let it carry you away."

"But, Dad — well, see, things have been happening," Lynne blurted out. "It's really scary. Something is weird in this house, Dad."

Caitlin felt annoyed with her sister. She was not sure this was the time or place to tell their father about the ghosts.

But Lynne had already opened her big mouth, Caitlin thought. There was no choice now.

"Dad, Lynne's right," she said. "All kinds of things have been happening. Doors have been opening by themselves and clothes I've hung in the closet have been getting packed back in boxes."

Caitlin realized how ridiculous this sounded, but there was no turning back now. She pressed ahead with her explanation.

"And the heat was shut off by itself and — "

"Wait, wait, wait. Hold on here, girls," their father replied. "This all sounds like something you saw on TV or read in one of those *Shivers* books. Now just stop and think about it. How could these things really happen?"

"But, Dad — you said yourself that the knife seemed to jump out of the drawer and cut you," Caitlin answered.

"And Dad, remember the dirt that almost fell on top of Caitlin and I? How did that happen?" Lynne said.

"Caitlin and *me*," their father corrected.

"Whatever. But Dad, you don't get it! This is serious," Lynne answered.

"It's true, Dad. For once, Lynne is right. There is something really wrong with this house," Caitlin said, trying to get up the nerve to say the word to her father.

The same word she did not want to say out loud to her sister. The scary "G" word.

"Ghosts, Dad!" she said, finally. "Ghosts! We have a house haunted by ghosts!"

Their father laughed.

"Look, girls. If you want to scare yourselves, that's fine," he said. "But you're being silly and I think you're both old enough to know it. Now I have some things to finish outside before it gets dark. We can talk about all this later — at dinner."

"But, *Daaaaad* — " Caitlin whined.

"But, *Daaaaad* — " Lynne whined at the same time.

Their father laughed again, waving his hand at them as he walked out the door.

"Good-bye, girls," he said with an amused snort. "Do me a favor and wash all that silverware before you put it in the drawer again, will you? I swear, I don't know where you two get your imaginations. I think you're both going to grow up to be writers or something. You can tell me more ghost stories later if you want to!"

And, still grinning, he closed the door behind him.

"You stupid little kid!" Caitlin said, slapping Lynne's arm. "Why did you have to say something about the ghosts when Dad was busy? Now he'll never believe us! He's going to have to see the strange things happen for himself!"

"Don't call me stupid! Dad told you never to say that to me," Lynne responded. "Besides, what's the difference when we told him? He would never believe some dumb story like this anyway! He's a scientist. Scientists don't believe in ghosts!"

"Well come on, let's pick up all this stuff on the floor and — "

But Caitlin stopped in the middle of her sentence.

Her mouth fell open in shock. And fear.

Lynne's mouth hung wide open, too.

Because when the girls stopped arguing and turned around to face the spilled silverware, the silverware was gone.

A single cardboard box on the floor had taken the place of the knives and forks and spoons.

The small box was closed. It was sealed with heavy packing tape.

And a sticker on top of it said, "Silverware."

In the few moments the sisters had turned their backs, the family's silverware had been packed back inside a moving company box.

As if some ghost or some monster or some troll who lived in the basement — as if *something*, at any rate — wanted the family to pack all their boxes and leave this old house forever.

Chapter Nine

During dinner, Caitlin's mother and father had a good laugh about the ghosts.

"You really do have quite the gift for fantasy, my dear," her mother told her.

"It's great that your mind is so creative, honey," her father said. "But as I told you earlier, don't let your thoughts get so carried away that you scare yourself with them. And you're scaring your little sister, too. That's not right."

"Dad, Cait isn't imagining things. That box of silverware got all packed up on its own," Lynne replied, trying to defend her sister.

"Well, I wish those ghosts would *unpack* our boxes instead of packing them up," their mother said with a laugh. "Now *that* would be useful!"

"Mom, Dad — please! Try to listen to me for a

change," Caitlin begged. "I know I'm just a twelve-year-old kid and everything, but I am not imagining this stuff! This is not something I've made up or read in a book or seen on TV. It is real! Our house is haunted!"

"Then why haven't your mother and I seen any evidence of these so-called ghosts, Caitlin? In science, we learn that you do not believe in anything until you can prove its existence," their father answered. "Not one strange thing has happened to us. Nothing unusual has taken place in our presence. I think you're just worked up because of the move — and your mind is playing tricks on you."

"I mean, really, darling," their mother said casually. "We wouldn't be going out tonight if we thought this place was truly haunted."

"Going *out*?" Caitlin asked.

"Going *out*?" Lynne asked, at the same time.

"Yes. Going out," their father said. "We have been invited over to one of our new neighbor's homes for the evening. It's just several houses away from here. But we will be out rather late, I think. So you girls will have to get yourselves to bed on time."

"But, *Daaad*! What about the *ghosts?*" Lynne whined.

"Dad, please! I know I said I'm too old for a baby-sitter, but I do not want to be alone with Lynne in this house tonight," Caitlin said. "I'm really scared, Dad! There *are* ghosts in this house!"

"For the last time, girls. There are *no* ghosts in this house — or anywhere else for that matter," their father said firmly. "Now I expect you both to behave as grown-ups tonight and take care of each other. Have fun, watch some TV in your new home. And stop worrying about ghosts!"

"And get to bed by ten at the latest. Both of you," their mother added. "We need you to help clean up and unpack around the house tomorrow. You'll need your rest."

There was no point in arguing any more, Caitlin understood. Her parents were going to visit neighbors for the whole evening — and there was nothing anyone could do to stop them. She and Lynne would be alone in the house.

Alone.

With the ghosts.

Caitlin and Lynne got together before their parents left. The girls made a sacred pact as sisters: They agreed to stick together through the night, no matter what happened.

They would not try to scare each other as a joke. They would not leave each other alone for more than a few moments.

And if they had to, they would fight the ghosts together.

When it was almost eight, and their parents were walking out the front door, Caitlin and Lynne kissed them both on the cheek. They told their parents to have fun. And they stood in the door, waving good-bye.

They hoped it would not be the last good-bye they ever waved to their parents.

Caitlin closed the door and looked at her sister. Neither said a word.

They walked toward the kitchen to make popcorn.

They had decided to watch a Disney video to distract themselves, and make them feel better. Maybe popcorn and Mary Poppins would make the ghosts stay away.

"Shouldn't we lock the door first, Cait?" Lynne asked. She glanced at the deadbolt.

"*No! No!*" Caitlin said. "I'm not worried about locking anything out tonight. I'm worried about being locked *in* with ghosts!"

At that exact moment, a blood-chilling howl echoed up from the basement.

Mmmmmwwwwwwwooooooooooaaaaaaaaaaahh hhhhhhhhhhhh!

Terrified, the sisters stared at each other. Their eyes were as wide as saucers. Lynne shook with fear. Caitlin could not move at all.

And then they heard another sound. And this one was even more frightening.

It was the sound of the doors locking — all by themselves!

One by one, the heavy metal locks slammed shut.

First the front door: *Gggwwaaccckk!*

Then the back door: *Gggwwaaccckk!*

Then the door to the garage: *Gggwwaaccckk!*

Then every window locked itself, one after another after another, all around the old home: *Ppphhheewwwtt! Ppphhheewwwtt! Ppphhheewwwtt! Ppphhheewwwtt! Ppphhheewwwtt!*

Caitlin ran to the front door, hoping to force it open before it was too late.

It was already locked!

She grabbed and twisted the deadbolt lock — but she could not budge it.

She wrestled frantically with the door handle, yanking and jiggling it with all her strength.

No use!

Caitlin and Lynne were locked inside this strange, horrifying, haunted house!

With no one to help them!

And no place to hide!

And no way out!

Chapter Ten

"We can't panic, Lynn!" Caitlin said, but the quaver in her voice betrayed her own fear. "Let's use our heads. We've got think how to deal with this!"

"Cait, I'm scared," Lynne cried. Tears streamed down her cheeks. "What is going to happen to us?"

"Nothing! Remember what the book said? Ghosts don't injure or kill people. They only cause fear and misery," Caitlin said. "All we have to do is *not* be afraid, no matter what happens. And just wait for Mom and Dad to get home. Let's go call them. They left the number for us, remember?"

"I wish they were here now," Lynne whined. "I really do not like this house."

They tried the telephone in the front hallway.

The phone was dead. It was as if the line to the

house had been cut.

Caitlin and Lynne walked nervously, hand in hand, through the living room, down the hallway toward the kitchen.

The ghosts were only trying to frighten them, Caitlin kept reminding her sister. She was trying to convince herself at the same time. If she said it over and over and over, in a firm enough voice, maybe she would find a way to believe it.

"The only thing we need is courage," she said. "Just don't be afraid and nothing can happen. Ghosts cannot hurt us!"

And so together, still holding hands tightly, the two girls pushed open the heavy door and walked into the kitchen.

But this time, there was no squeak from the door.

Instead, there was a long, low, whining wail — spooky and shrill.

Eeeeeeeeeeeeeeeeeeeeeeeaaaaaaaaaaaaaaarrrrrrr rrrr!

And when the wail began, the doorknob started to shake in Caitlin's hand until the whole door rattled and vibrated wildly.

Caitlin tried to hold on to the knob, but couldn't.

The door pulled loose from her hand — and swung back toward the girls.

Lynne jumped away but the door slammed into Caitlin's forehead, knocking her to the floor.

"Caitlin! Caitlin! Are you OK?" Lynne shouted, rushing to her sister's side. "Cait! Talk to me!"

Caitlin tried to shake off the pain, rubbing her forehead and moaning.

"Ooowwww! Yeah, I'm OK. I *guess*," she complained. "But my head hurts. Just let me rest here for a minute before I get up."

But there was no time for resting — or anything else.

Because now all the cabinets and all the drawers in the kitchen began to open and close by themselves. Rapidly and loudly, each one opened and shut, opened and shut — without a human hand touching them!

Kkklaaacckk! went every cabinet.

Vhhhoooot! went every drawer.

*Kkklaaacckk!   Vhhhoooot!   Kkklaaacckk!
Vhhhoooot! Kkklaaacckk! Vhhhoooot!*

It resembled a scene from a nightmare — loud and shocking!

Caitlin was too afraid to feel her bump on the head. Too afraid to do anything!

This, she knew, was no nightmare. This was a very dangerous reality.

Suddenly, a drawer blasted out of a kitchen counter, like a cannonball fired in a battle.

It hurled itself right at Caitlin and Lynne.

They watched, frozen in horror, as this kitchen missile sailed across the room toward them! Directly at their heads!

And as the drawer took dead aim at their skulls, the girls did the only thing they could think to do at that awful moment.

Together, in perfect unison, they screamed!

Aaaaaaaaaaaaaaaaaaaaaaaaahhhhhhhhhh!!!!

Chapter Eleven

The kitchen drawer was bearing down on their heads!

At the last moment, it seemed to get an extra boost of power from somewhere. It roared harmlessly over the sisters' heads!

They heard the drawer whistle past their ears and explode into a thousand splinters against the kitchen door behind them.

The splinters dropped around them like rain.

"Run, Lynne!" Caitlin shouted. "Run for your life!"

She grabbed Lynne's hand and dragged her out of the kitchen, through the long hall and up the stairs. They raced into Caitlin's room and shut the door behind them, locking it.

Lynne was crying. Tears streamed down her

cheeks. Her eyes were wide with fear, her nose was running, and she was shaking like a leaf.

"Caitlin, what can we do? What's happening?" she wailed, between sobs. "We were almost *killed* by that drawer!"

Caitlin fumbled around her desk for the book about ghosts, goblins and ghouls. There *must* be some explanation for what was going on inside their house!

Horrible things were happening! Dangerous things! Maybe even deadly things!

This did not seem like ghosts anymore . . .

"Cait, what are you *doing*!" Lynne shouted. "We have to get out of here right now! Why are you reading that stupid book?"

"I just need to find something, Lynne. Shhh! Be quiet a second! Let me read," Caitlin snapped.

Scanning the book as quickly as she could, Caitlin flipped through page after page after page. The pages shook and rustled as she turned them with her trembling fingers.

If these were not ghosts in the house, what were they?

Maybe once the sisters knew what was attacking them they could find a way to fight back.

Caitlin poured through the frightening ghost book, scanning pages and pages and pages, reading as rapidly as possible.

She saw nothing that could explain anything that had happened to them.

Until she got to the very last page.

She read the words slowly, carefully. As she read, her heart beat faster and faster. A cold shudder of fear made her hands shake so hard she could barely finish reading.

Caitlin looked up at her sister. Their eyes met. Both of them dreaded facing the truth.

"Wh-what? What is it?" Lynne asked.

"I know what's wrong with the house, Lynne," Caitlin said quietly, as though she felt they were doomed. "It hardly ever happens anywhere. But when it does happen, it's even worse than having ghosts! *A lot* worse!"

"Wh-what do, uh, you mean — uh, worse?" Lynne stammered, almost unable to speak.

"There are no ghosts out to hurt us, Lynne. It's the *house* that's trying to get rid of us," Caitlin said. "Our family moved into a house that hates people. It despises anyone living inside its walls. The house wants to force us to leave."

"The house hates people?" Lynne asked, starting to cry again. "What does that mean, Cait? What does that mean?"

"It means this house fights a war against anyone who tries to live here," Caitlin answered. "And it will do anything it has to do. Our own home would kill our whole family just to make us go away!"

Chapter Twelve

"Caitlin, that doesn't make any sense!" Lynne bawled. "How can a house attack anybody all by itself?"

"The book says houses have personalities, just like people, Lynne. And sometimes, a house gets mean," Caitlin said. "Here, listen. I'll read part of it to you."

"*There is an important distinction between a haunted house and a **haunting** house. The haunted house is troubled only by ghosts, which may frighten the human occupants but never will harm them. However, in a haunting house, anyone who lives in the dwelling is in grave danger,*" Caitlin read to her sister.

"*Hauntings are very rare. They come only to homes that are old and unwanted. It helps to think of haunting houses as similar to old angry men who want no one living nearby. The buildings become like hermits, resenting the human race for ignoring them. When humans attempt to move in, a haunting house comes alive. The wood and brick and glass and metal take on a life of their own, suddenly possessed by a violent force. (However, a haunting house has only very limited power over objects owned by the residents — these objects cannot be used for violence.)*

"Instead, the house itself wages a war. It produces strange sounds from furnaces or door hinges or anything else that may frighten people. And the house will use doors or windows or any other weapons at its disposal to physically attack the residents, harming or killing the unfortunate occupants."

"I hate this house!" Lynne yelled. "I hate it! I hate it!"

"I hate it, too!" Caitlin said. "But we've got to figure some way to get out of here right now or we'll never live through this night! I don't think we have much time to waste!"

"Does the book say how to make the house stop attacking us, Caitlin?" Lynne asked. "Or maybe it tells us how to get out? Then we can run down the road and get Mom and Dad!"

Caitlin glanced sadly at her sister, shaking her head. Then she looked down at the book and read from it again:

"There is no known way to rid a haunting house of its violent forces. The only way to survive is for the residents to leave quickly," the book said. *"Only a fortunate few have ever escaped a haunting house once the building has launched a full-fledged attack. Typically, the house will lock all the doors and windows. After that, the house will destroy any living thing left inside!"*

"What are we going to do?" Lynne said, starting to cry again. "We're going to be killed by our own house!"

"No, we're not!" Caitlin answered. "Come on, Lynne. Hurry up! I have an idea! And stop crying, will you? We have to be calm if we're going to find a way to get out of here!"

Holding Lynne's hand, she hurried downstairs and stood in front of a living room window.

Then she looked around for something heavy. She spotted a large lamp on an end table. It was her mother's favorite lamp but that didn't matter now.

If she didn't do something, her mother might never see either of her daughters alive again!

Without hesitating, Caitlin picked up the lamp and threw it through the window. The window glass shattered, falling on to the front lawn.

Now there was a big hole in the window — easily big enough for two young girls to crawl through.

It was their only possible way out of the house.

"Hurry, Lynne!" Caitlin shouted. "Get outside! I'll be right behind you! Just watch out for those sharp pieces of glass still hanging from the window!"

Caitlin watched as her sister scampered to the window and put one leg through the opening to the ledge outside. The ledge was littered with dirt and small pebbles, and Lynne tried to kick them aside to find a firm foothold.

All she had to do now was squeeze her body around the sharp glass and she would be safe.

But escape was not going to be so simple. Not with the deadly house watching every move!

Just as Lynne was about to crawl outside, the

window quickly unlocked itself — and suddenly began to open.

"Lynne, look out!" Caitlin screamed.

Huge shards of glass were pointed at Lynne. They were moving fast — very fast — toward her neck!

Caitlin felt helpless as the window flung itself open.

Her little sister was about to have her throat cut by a window full of jagged glass!

Chapter Thirteen

As the razor-sharp glass sliced toward Lynne's throat, her foot suddenly lost its grip on the window ledge.

She slipped on a small pebble, tumbling back inside the house as though she had stepped on a banana peel.

She flopped to the living room floor a split second before the window slammed all the way up. The sharp glass whooshed by her, cutting only air.

A tiny stone under her foot had saved Lynne from being carved into ribbons.

"Lynne! Are you hurt?" Caitlin asked, helping her sister off the floor. "I thought you were finished that time for sure!"

"Wow, another close one, huh? If I hadn't slipped on the ledge, I never could have moved out of the way in time," Lynne panted, looking at the window. "Hey, look, Caitlin! The window's open now. Come on! Let's jump outside and get out of here! Quick!"

But before they could get close, the window began to slide forcefully up and down, up and down, up and down. It would cut or crush anyone who tried to get through.

"There's no way, Lynne. We'll never make it outside!" Caitlin said.

The situation looked desperate. They were doomed if they stayed inside the house — and doomed if they tried to escape.

Caitlin tried to stay calm and think. Panicking would not help them now.

Suddenly, she brightened.

"I just thought of something else," she said. "The window's broken open! We can yell for help! Maybe someone will hear us!"

"The houses are all so far apart here, Cait. No one will hear anything! And besides, we're at the end of the road!" Lynne worried.

"We have to try! Come on!" Caitlin said

firmly. "Yell like your life depends on it. Because it does!"

And so the two girls stood peering out the broken window, which still rose and fell and rose and fell on its own. And they began to shout.

"Heeeelllpp!" Caitlin bellowed.

"Hhhheeeeeeeeellllllllpp!" Lynne yelled.

No sooner had the first sounds come from their lips than a pair of shutters slapped closed over the window.

Thhwwaaaaaaaaappp! Thhhwwwaaaaaaaappp!

And then heavy wood shutters slammed tight over every other window in the house. Caitlin and Lynne could hear them banging shut everywhere, sealing the sisters even more tightly inside the killer house.

Thhwwaaapp! Thhwwaaapp! Thhwwaaapp! Thhwwaaapp! Thhwwaaapp!

"There's no way to get out now, Cait! There's nothing we can do," Lynne said.

She fought back her tears bravely, but fear still showed in her eyes.

"We're not going to give up, Lynne! We can't!

Mom and Dad wouldn't give up if they were here," Caitlin said. "We have to think of some way to beat this old, rotten, stinking house!"

"I hate this house!" Lynne said angrily.

"There must be *something* we can do!" Caitlin said.

She pressed her hands to her forehead, thinking as hard as she could.

At last, she got an idea . . .

But it was an idea that she did not like.

An idea that sent icy chills of terror up her spine.

They would have to go into the basement to look for a way out, Caitlin explained — into the dark, damp, cold, frightening basement.

In the best of times, walking into the basement felt like walking inside a large grave. And these were not the best of times.

But Caitlin insisted.

"Dad might have some tools down there we can use to break through the doors," she said. "Maybe he has an ax or something. *Anything!* We might be able to break out of here before the house murders us!"

"No way! *I'm* not going into that basement! Especially not now," Lynne said. "Nope, Caitlin! Sorry! Not me! No *way!*"

"Way!" Caitlin said. "We *have* to, Lynne!"

After several minutes of heavy convincing, Lynne finally agreed. The basement was their only hope.

With Caitlin leading the way, the girls opened the thick, squeaking door to the basement. They flicked on the switch. One dim bulb that hung on a wire from the ceiling spread a wavering and gloomy glow around the basement.

They took one step onto the wooden stairs that led down. The stair creaked loudly.

Rrrrrrrrrrrrrrrrrreeeeeeeeeeeeeeaaaaaaaaa!

They took another slow step.

Rrrrrrrrrrrrrrrrrreeeeeeeeeeeeeeaaaaaaaaa!

And another.

Rrrrrrrrrrrrrrrrrrrrrreeeeeeeeeeeeeeeeeeaaaa aaaaa!

The sisters were huddled together on the third of 13 steps into the basement when it happened.

The door behind them flung itself closed. At the same instant, the basement light went out.

It was completely black now, without even the faintest light shining under the basement door.

They f 't as if they were shut inside a huge tomb.

"Aaaaaaahhh! We're trapped in the basement!" Lynne screamed. She began to sob uncontrollably. "We're going to die! We're going to be killed by something we can't even see!"

Chapter Fourteen

"Stop crying, Lynne! Stop it!" Caitlin ordered. "It doesn't help anything! And stop saying we're going to die! I know we can find a way out of here! Just wait. Stand right there!"

Caitlin carefully creaked back up the stairs, feeling her way through the darkness to the basement door. Neither girl could see anything at all.

The door squeaked as Caitlin pushed on it. But it opened. Now, however, the rest of the house was also shrouded in darkness.

"We're not locked in the basement, Lynne. The door's open. Come on back up here," Caitlin said. "There is no lock on this door. But it looks like all the lights are out in the whole house. We'll have to find Dad's flashlight."

Caitlin and Lynne stumbled their way into the

kitchen, where they found a box containing a long silver flashlight, a candle, and matches.

The house was pitch black. The heavy shutters prevented nearly all the pale moonlight from leaking in through the windows. It was almost impossible to see anything.

They turned on the flashlight, lit the candle and walked back to the basement steps. Caitlin held the flashlight. Lynne carried the candle.

They both knew what they had to do. They *had* to go back down those basement steps.

No matter how scared they were.

The tool they needed was in the basement — and it was their only chance to break out of the house and find their parents.

Step by creaky step, surrounded by darkness, the two girls walked down the old wooden staircase toward the basement.

Rrrrrrrrrrrrrrreeeeeeeeeeeeeeeaaaaaaaaaaa!

After every step or two, Caitlin and Lynne turned to look at each other, as if to make sure someone friendly was still standing close.

Rrrrrrrrrrrrrrreeeeeeeeeeeeeeeaaaaaaaaaaaa!

Rrrrrrrrrrrrrreeeeeeeeeeeeeeaaaaaaaaaa!

Finally, after thirteen frightening steps, they reached the basement floor.

"Uh, I — uh, well, I don't know — uh, if this was such a good idea," Lynne stammered.

"Yeah, I — I, uh, know what you mean," Caitlin stammered back.

The basement was the scariest place either girl had ever been.

There was something about the total blackness of the damp cellar, pierced only by a single flashlight and a single candle.

And there was something about the look of the room: Spider webs dangled from the wooden beams overhead. Water dripped from an old boiler. Black bugs crawled across the cold concrete walls.

And there was something about standing in the bottom of a house that was plotting to murder them!

This was a very dangerous place, and both sisters knew it.

"L-let's, uh, get out of here, Caitlin!" Lynne said nervously. "Something bad is going to happen if we stay in this basement!"

"Uh, yeah, OK, Lynne. B-but, let's find an ax or something first," Caitlin said just as nervously. "Dad must h-have something like that in his tools. We, uh, we have to find some way to knock down the door. Or we'll be stuck in this house forever!"

"I, uh — I don't, uh, know, Caitlin," Lynne answered. "But I guess you're, uh, right."

And then, from somewhere, came a loud, horrifying howl:

Mmmmmwwwwwwwoooooooooaaaaaaaahhhhhhhhhhh!

It sounded like the wail of one very large, very angry bear!

Both girls screamed. They jumped back as far as they could jump, and grabbed each other.

Lynne dropped the candle. The flame went out.

Caitlin just managed to hang on to the flashlight as she hugged her sister.

Then Caitlin understood where the howl was coming from.

"Lynne, listen. It's just the boiler. Remember, like the book said — the house will make any sounds it can to scare people," Caitlin said. "It's the same thing we heard before, upstairs, only now we're standing right next to it. It's just that poor old boiler giving off a spooky sound to frighten us. That thing looks so old, I almost feel sorry for it. Come on, let's find Dad's tools and get out of here."

As Caitlin explained, the sound somehow abruptly stopped.

With only the flashlight to light their way, Caitlin and Lynne began to search the stacks of boxes.

Where was the box marked "Tools?" It had to be somewhere.

Caitlin had never paid much attention to her father's tools before. But he must own something that would break down a wooden door, she thought. And it must be inside one of these boxes.

The flashlight beam shone around the black basement as Caitlin searched for any sign of the tools.

"Oh, no!" she said. "Oh, no!"

"What? What is it, Cait?" Lynne asked.

"Look! Look where the tools are," Caitlin said. She pointed high overhead.

The cardboard box marked "Tools" was sitting

on the tallest shelf in the basement — far out of their reach.

"Dad would never have put that box up there," Lynne said.

"No, and he didn't! The *house* moved it up there," Caitlin said. "The book says a haunting house has limited power over our belongings, remember? The house can't hurt us with anything we own — but it can sure make our things move around a lot!"

The girls did not give up, though. They came up with a plan to get into the box of tools anyway.

Caitlin got on her hands and knees, ignoring the clammy feeling of the cold, wet basement floor. Lynne stepped on her sister's back, flailing at the box with the flashlight.

If Lynne hit the box with the flashlight hard enough, Caitlin said, the tools might fall to the ground.

Lynne swung at the box and missed. She swung again and hit it. The heavy box hardly budged.

"Hit it again! Hit it harder!" Caitlin urged.

"I *hate* this house!" Lynne said, swinging wildly at the box.

Just then, there was a noise.

A noise neither girl had heard before.

A noise like heavy wood bending and cracking and breaking.

"What's that?" Caitlin asked. "Shine your light around and see if you see anything, Lynne!"

Lynne did as she was told.

What she saw in the beam of light made her gasp in horror!

"Cait!" Lynne screamed. "Cait, *look*!"

One of the enormous wooden beams that held up the floor of the house was cracking in half — right above them.

The entire house was about to fall on top of the terrified sisters, crushing them under two tons of wood and brick and metal!

Chapter Fifteen

The crack in the beam was spreading.

The thick, square piece of wood began to sag in the middle.

Soon the entire house would plummet into the basement, killing anything under it.

Lynne froze with panic. She stood stock still, shining the flashlight on the beam. She could not even cry.

Despite the danger, Caitlin somehow stayed calm.

In an instant, she sized up how big the crack was, how fast it was spreading, and where, exactly, the beam lay under the floor.

She understood they still had a chance to survive.

But only if they moved together. *Now!*

"Jump, Lynne! Jump," Caitlin shouted.

She hoped her sister would react without thinking.

Lynne leaped off her sister's back, exactly as Caitlin had hoped.

"Now hold on to that flashlight!" Caitlin said.

Pulling her sister's arm, she bolted for the staircase. She could barely see because Lynne pointed the flashlight toward the floor.

But she could see just enough.

Spotting the outline of the staircase, she raced up the creaky stairs two at a time. She felt stronger than she had ever been before, almost as if she could lift her sister up the stairs.

The girls bounded up the steps until they reached the basement door.

It had closed itself again, but that was no problem, Caitlin remembered. The basement door had no lock.

If they got off the staircase before the beam broke, probably they would be safe. The kitchen floor would collapse into the basement, Caitlin understood — but the rest of the house should remain standing.

Caitlin pushed against the door.

It would not open. It had no lock but still it would not open. It seemed the house had found some way to lock the door anyway.

Maybe the killer house finally had discovered a foolproof plan for murder!

Caitlin pushed and shoved against the door. Desperately, she pounded it with her shoulder.

But the door was still shut tight.

The sound of the beam breaking grew louder and louder.

Remembering how strong her tomboy sister could be, Caitlin pulled Lynne up to the top step.

"Help me get the door open, Lynne! Push! Push! Push!" Caitlin screamed.

Together, they hammered against the heavy door.

"Push! Push!" Caitlin yelled.

Again and again, they pounded on the door.

At last the door popped open.

But it opened at the very moment the beam snapped in half with a deafening crack and crash.

Everything in the kitchen — the tables and

chairs and cabinets and drawers and boxes — exploded into the basement with a thunderous boom!

Dust and smoke billowed everywhere, as if a bomb had gone off.

As the kitchen tumbled into the basement, the staircase collapsed under the girls' feet!

Caitlin and Lynne grabbed on to the hallway floor and hung on with all their strength — their bodies half inside the open basement door, half outside.

Their shoulders and heads were on the first floor. Their legs and feet dangled toward the ruins of the basement.

Every other part of their bodies struggled to keep from falling.

Beneath them now was nothing but a long drop into a deep hole — into a pit filled with sharp debris from the kitchen.

"Hang on, Lynne!" Caitlin shouted. "Hang on with everything you've got!"

Caitlin could feel her own fingers beginning to slip, though. She reached for the doorway but it was no good.

She could not hold on to anything much longer!

Within seconds, Caitlin realized, she would fall helplessly to her death in the basement below!

Chapter Sixteen

Caitlin's fingers were sliding off the wooden door frame.

Slip — a quarter-inch.

Slip — a half-inch.

Slip — another half-inch.

Slip! — an inch.

Little by little, Caitlin was starting to fall.

At the same time, Lynne struggled to pull herself up, wriggling her legs and using all the muscles in her strong, tomboy arms.

With one last determined effort, she hoisted her body on to the hallway floor.

"*Aaaaaaaaagh!*" she said as her arms strained under the weight.

She lay on the floor, safe but panting from exhaustion.

Then she heard Caitlin's frightened little cry for help. She saw that her sister could not hold on more than a second or two longer.

"Ohhhhh," Caitlin said, her voice like a soft squeal. "Ohhh, Lynnnne."

Lynne hopped to her feet and grabbed Caitlin's arms just as her fingers slipped off the door frame.

She caught Caitlin and pulled hard.

She braced her legs against the door frame for support, tugging and yanking on Caitlin's arms.

Caitlin was heavy, much heavier than Lynne. For a moment, it looked as if Lynne would not be able to save her sister, no matter how hard she tried.

Her arms shook. Her face turned red. Her legs wobbled.

But she held on tightly.

"*Aaaaaaaaaggghh!*" she grunted. "Don't give up, Cait! Hold on!"

The thought of Caitlin falling into the basement gave Lynne more strength than she had ever had before. She summoned all her effort for one last heave. She leaned back and pulled with all her might.

At last she dragged her sister into the hallway.

"Are you all right, Cait?" she asked, breathing even more heavily than before. "I was so afraid! I wasn't sure I could pull you up."

"You did it! You saved our lives!" Caitlin said. "You really were brave! You never quit trying! I will never call you a little kid again!"

They lay on the floor, tired and scared and confused.

What should they do now?

It seemed as if there was no hope.

Even though the kitchen floor had collapsed, the walls of the home had remained intact.

The tools, of course, were buried under tons of debris. The doors and windows were locked and sealed shut.

There still was no way out of the killer house.

The phones did not work. The lights were all off. Even the flashlight was gone — Lynne had dropped it when the staircase collapsed.

And their parents would not be home for hours.

The girls knew they could not wait for Mom and Dad to rescue them. By the time their parents came home, they would be dead.

"Cait, I just thought of something," Lynne said. "There's this thing in my room I didn't tell you about. Something cool I found. Maybe it's a way out."

"Huh? What do you mean, Lynne? What's so special about your room?" Caitlin asked.

"Well, I — I didn't tell you about this before because I thought you would try to make me switch bedrooms," Lynne explained. "See, there's this little passageway. It's almost like a small tunnel. I found the opening behind an old board in the back of my closet."

"A secret tunnel? In this house? Are you kidding me, Lynne?" Caitlin replied.

"No, honest! It's the truth, Caitlin!" Lynne said. "It's pretty small and I haven't tried to crawl through it yet to find out where it goes. I just hid some letters and, well, a diary in there behind the board."

"A diary! You keep a diary?" Caitlin said, surprised. "My little sister has a diary!"

"Oh, stop it, Cait! We don't have time to play around. Yes, I have a diary. So what? Just don't ever touch it!" Lynne said. "But I think we should find out where this passageway goes, Cait. It might take us outside the house. Who knows?"

The sisters' eyes had adjusted to the blackness around them. Just enough moonlight seeped in through the shutters to allow them to see dimly where they were going.

They hurried through the darkened house up the stairs to Lynne's room. They stood looking into the small secret tunnel hidden in the back of Lynne's closet.

"Wow," Caitlin said. "It really *is* a passageway. It's hard to see in this light — but it looks like it might be a tunnel that goes somewhere. We have to try."

"But, Cait — you're too big to fit through the tunnel. I have to go by myself. I'm the only one small enough to crawl through," Lynne said.

"You can't go crawling around through secret tunnels by yourself! You're my little sister. I have to make sure you don't hurt yourself," Caitlin said. "I'll just have to find some way to fit through there, too."

"No way, Cait! Look how small it is! I have to go alone. Please let me go! *Pleeeaase!*" Lynne pleaded. "It may be the last chance we have to get out of this horrible house!"

Reluctantly, *very* reluctantly, Caitlin agreed with her sister.

The tunnel at least offered some hope of escaping the deadly home.

Lynne kissed her on the cheek. For the first time this night, Caitlin allowed herself to cry.

"Bye, Cait!" Lynne said. "If I find some way out, I'll run for Mom and Dad. And we'll come back to smash down the doors and get you out, too!"

Caitlin brushed away her tears and held her breath as Lynne got down on hands and knees, and began crawling off into the blackness.

Caitlin thought that a small tunnel was probably a very bad place to be in a house that was trying to kill people.

She did not want to let Lynne go. But she *had* to.

As she watched the pair of small feet disappear into the dark, uncertain passageway, she began to cry again. She just could not make the tears stop.

"I may never see my sister again," she whispered to herself.

Chapter Seventeen

Caitlin could still hear the sound of hands and knees and feet shuffling across the floor inside the tunnel.

She wanted desperately to know that her little sister was all right. Since she could hear her shuffling, she figured she could keep talking to her, and reassure herself that way.

"Lynne, can you hear me?" she called into the tunnel. "Answer if you can hear me."

"Yeah, I can hear you," Lynne said, her words echoing through the small opening.

"Keep talking to me, Lynne! I want you to tell me what you're doing and seeing as you crawl through there! OK?" Caitlin said.

"Sure, but there's not much to tell you," Lynne answered. "I can't see *anything*! It's completely black inside here. And I just keep going and going. I don't know how far this tunnel will go. I just hope it takes me to the garage or someplace where I can get outside!"

"Just talk about anything! I only want to know that you're safe! You just keep talking to me!" Caitlin ordered.

"OK," Lynne said. "So far, this is just a long, empty tunnel. I'm starting to wonder if it goes anywhere. Maybe it just goes through the walls — you know, so repairmen can get to the electric wires or water pipes or something."

Lynne's voice sounded fainter now, and more wrapped in echo upon echo. She was getting farther and farther away.

"Lynne, talk louder! It's getting hard to hear you!" Caitlin said.

"Yeah, OK. The tunnel is turning now. It's going off to the right — toward your room, I think," Lynne said. Then her tone changed to disgust. "Aaaaaww, no!"

"What? What happened?" Caitlin called anxiously.

"Nothing. I'm OK. I just put my hand down and felt some dead bug. Yuck!" Lynne replied.

"Just keep moving, Lynne. Keep moving as fast as you can! I want you to get out of that tunnel as quickly as possible! It's too dangerous in there!" Caitlin said.

"I'm hurrying, Cait! Believe me, I'm hurrying!" Lynne said.

Lynne's voice grew still fainter. Caitlin thought her sister must be a long way off.

For a short time, Caitlin heard nothing. She began to worry.

"Lynne, keep talking to me! I don't care what you say. Just talk!" she said.

She heard only silence.

Suddenly, the silence was shattered by a loud yell from the tunnel.

"Eeeeeeeaaaaaaahhh! Oh, no! Cait! Oh, no!" Lynne shouted.

"Lynne, what's wrong? Talk to me? Where are you?" Caitlin hollered back.

"Oh, it's just — *Pew! Pah! Phhhhttth!* It's so gross!" Lynne cried out to her sister. "Cockroaches,

Cait! Hundreds of cockroaches! They're crawling all over me! Oh, noooo! *Phhhhttth! Pew! Pah!* Oh, gross! I hate this house!"

Caitlin hated bugs. But she knew Lynne hated bugs even more.

Lynne despised bugs.

Caitlin could imagine how frightened and upset her sister must feel, surrounded by swarms of little bug-legs inside a dark tunnel!

"Come back, Lynne! Come back! Get out of there right now!" Caitlin shouted.

"No, it's OK, Cait! It was pretty gross but I'm OK now. They're gone," Lynne said. "Besides, I *can't* come back! The tunnel's too small for me to turn around. And I don't think I can crawl backward that far. I have to keep going!"

"You sound really far away, Lynne! Talk louder! I can barely hear you," Caitlin called.

"What do you want me to say?" Lynne asked.

"I don't care! I told you — just say *anything*! Talk real loud and say anything! I want to hear your voice!" Caitlin answered.

"OK, OK! Then I'll just say I really hope I do

not run into any more bugs, Caitlin! That was awful! I hate bugs!" Lynne said loudly. "And I *hate this house*! I hate it! I hate it! I hate it!"

"Yeah, just keep talking!" Caitlin reminded her.

There was a brief silence.

"Lynne? Lynne, are you all right?"

"Uh, Ca-Caitlin? Caitlin! Uh, this is really going to sound weird bu-but I think — " Lynne stammered.

"What? What's wrong now? What's happening in there, Lynne?" Caitlin called fearfully.

Was it another dead bug, Caitlin wondered. Was it another gross attack of cockroaches? Was it something worse — a mouse maybe? Or a rat? Or something even worse than that?

"*Aaaaaaaaaaaaaaaaaaaaaaaaaaahhhhhhhhh*!"

The scream was so loud and so horrifying that it turned Caitlin's arms and legs into a mass of goose bumps. She wrapped her arms around herself and shivered.

"Lynne!" she hollered. "What's wrong? Is something in the tunnel with you?"

"Caitlin! Heeeeelllllpp! Heeeelllpp me, *please*!" Lynne screamed.

"Lynne, try to crawl back out to me! I can't come in!" Caitlin pleaded. "I'm too big!"

Lynne screamed again — this time even louder than before!

"*AAAAAAaaaaaaaaaaaaaaaaaaaaaaahhhhh hhhh*!"

"Lynne! Lynne! Tell me what's going on in that tunnel!" Caitlin shouted.

"The tunnel is moving! It's squeezing down on me from the top and bottom, Caitlin!" Lynne answered. "I can hardly move now! It's getting smaller! It's going to squash me, Cait! It's going to smash me flat as a pancake!"

Chapter Eighteen

Caitlin felt completely, totally, utterly helpless.

Lynne was about to be squeezed like a human tube of toothpaste — and Caitlin could not do a thing to help her sister escape!

But she could at least yell!

"Crawl, Lynne! If you can move at all, crawl as fast as you can! Find some way out of there right now!" she shouted.

Maybe Lynne could hear her. Maybe Lynne could still move inside the tunnel. Maybe Lynne could find a passage out if she crawled fast enough.

Caitlin listened at the tunnel opening. She listened very hard. But she heard nothing.

Not a word.

Not a sound.

Nothing.

"Lynne? Lynne! Say something!" she shouted into the tunnel. "Speak to me! Please!"

Still not one word.

Not one sound.

Nothing.

Then, from somewhere inside the house, the voice of a small girl echoed.

"Caitlin!" the distant voice said. "I'm faaaaaaalllling!"

It was Lynne's voice, very faint, very weak.

Lynne was saying she was falling!

But how? How could that possibly be?

Caitlin thought for a moment and decided Lynne had found some way to squeeze through the contracting tunnel. She had not been squashed after all.

Her sister was still alive!

But Caitlin also understood the tunnel must empty into a chute of some kind — and Lynne had fallen down it!

"That tunnel must drop inside the house somewhere," Caitlin said to herself. "Lynne's probably laying someplace right now, all crumpled up from her fall. She could be hurt!"

Caitlin knew she had to find her sister — fast!

Hurrying through the darkness, she descended the stairs and began the search. She started checking out the area where the kitchen had collapsed into the basement. She looked and listened carefully from the edge of the open pit but saw nothing and heard nothing.

Lynne had not tumbled into that pile of sharp kitchen debris. Thank goodness!

So, Caitlin decided, her sister must have fallen into one of the rooms on the ground floor.

She ran down the shadowy hallway to continue the hunt for Lynne.

She soon discovered it was going to be tougher than she had imagined.

The haunting house opened the heavy wooden door to each room — until the moment Caitlin approached.

As she rushed toward the dining room, the dining room door slammed shut in her face!

As she rushed toward the living room, the living room door slammed shut in her face!

As she rushed toward her father's study, the study door slammed shut in her face!

No matter how hard she yanked on the knobs, the doors would not open.

She pounded on the doors, calling Lynne's name.

Still she heard no sound.

Caitlin was now locked out of every room on the ground floor. Only the hallway and stairs and bedrooms were open to her.

But Lynne was trapped inside one of the downstairs rooms somewhere, hurt or maybe worse.

The situation was getting more terrifying every moment.

She was all alone. Her sister was wounded. And the house was closing in for the kill!

Then Caitlin saw something that made her scream.

Under the staircase, crumpled in a heap, lay Lynne.

Even through the heavy blackness of the old home, Caitlin noticed some thick liquid dripping from Lynne's arm.

A thick liquid that looked like blood!

And Caitlin noticed something even more terrible: Lynne was not moving, not even a finger.

And she did not seem to be breathing, either.

As far as Caitlin could tell, her wonderful, brave, sweet nine-year-old sister was dead!

The killer house had killed already!

Chapter Nineteen

"Oooohh, ow!" came a sound from under the staircase.

It was Lynne's voice.

She was alive!

"Lynne, are you hurt? Tell me if you're all right," Caitlin said, running to her sister's side.

Caitlin could see now that the liquid on her sister's arm was only some greasy water. Lynne was not bleeding after all.

"Ow, Cait. I fell and must have bumped my head. It's kind of sore. But I'm OK," Lynne answered slowly.

Caitlin understood that Lynne accidentally had found the other end of the narrow tunnel.

The black passageway that began in Lynne's bedroom had turned into nothing more than a hole —

a chute that plunged from the second floor to the ground.

The hole emptied into a space under the stairs. No one had ever noticed that space before because it was covered by a small, secret door — a door that looked just like part of the wall.

Luckily, a lot of old rags and sheets were there to soften Lynne's landing. When Lynne had fallen, she had bumped her head, knocked the door open and rolled out on to the floor under the stairs.

"There's still something I can't figure out, Lynne. Why didn't you get squashed when the tunnel began squeezing down on you? How did you get away?" Caitlin asked.

"I heard your voice telling me to crawl as fast as I could. So I did! I got down flat on the bottom of the tunnel and pulled myself forward with just my arms. I pulled really hard!" Lynne said. "I was lucky I got to the hole really quick and fell. The tunnel was so small I could barely move."

Caitlin helped Lynne stand up and asked again if she was hurt anywhere. Lynne said she was OK. Except for a headache.

Caitlin told Lynne everything that had just happened — the desperate search and the locked doors and the killer house closing in around them.

"What can we do, Cait? We can't last much longer," Lynne said.

Her voice trembled with terror.

"I just remembered something in your room, Lynne!" Caitlin answered, snapping her fingers. "I saw it in your closet when you went into the tunnel. You have a big metal softball bat in there! Maybe we can use it to bash through the front door and get outside!"

"Yeah! And even if we can't break through, maybe someone would hear the noise when we hit the door," Lynne said. "Then they'll send the police to save us!"

"Come on, Lynne! Let's go!" Caitlin shouted.

She grabbed her sister's hand and raced to the staircase. Together, they ran up the dark stairs and down the shadowy hall.

The door to every room on the second floor was open now. The girls hurried to reach Lynne's bedroom before anything else happened.

Maybe they still had a chance, if only they

could get to that softball bat, Caitlin thought.

But they would never find out.

It already was too late!

Just as they were about to run into Lynne's room, the door slammed shut in their faces.

"Oh, Cait!" Lynne cried, pulling on the door handle. "We can't get in! It's locked."

"We have got to find somewhere to hide out and plan what to do next," Caitlin said. "Follow me!"

Terrified, they rushed down the hall toward Caitlin's room. At least it was better to sit in there than to stand stranded in the hallway, Caitlin thought.

But again, it was too late!

As they tried to hurry into the bedroom, Caitlin's door slammed shut in their faces.

Maybe their parents' room would be the safest place. It was the only bedroom with a door still open and unlocked.

They tore down the hallway and tried to jump through the door in time.

But they were too late once more!

Their parents' door slammed shut in their faces.

"We're trapped!" Lynne shouted. "We're trapped in the hall! We have no place to run any more! No place to hide! No way to get out of the house! I hate this house! I hate it!"

"I don't hate it, Lynne," Caitlin said softly. "I feel sorry for this house."

"Huh? Sorry for it? What are you talking about, Cait? Are you crazy?" Lynne asked.

"If a house as big and strong and old as this one has to pick on two little girls, it's just sad. That's all, it's just sad!" Caitlin replied. "I feel really sorry for anybody or anything that likes to hurt people! We haven't done anything to this house! The only thing we've done is move here and try to fix it up and make it pretty again."

"But, Cait! This house is trying to kill us! How can you feel sorry for something so mean?" Lynne wondered. "It tried to bury us under dirt. It tried to hit us with flying drawers! It tried to cut my throat with broken glass! And then it almost crushed us in the basement! And don't forget everything else it did to us! And now we're stuck in the hall with no way out. How can you say that you don't hate this house?"

"I mean it, Lynne! I don't hate this house. I never really did," Caitlin explained. "I just didn't want to leave our old house, that's all. But really, I did want to be happy here with our family and find new friends and get along in our new school. I don't hate this house. But now we'll never get to live here with Mom and Dad because the house is going to kill us. I wish this house didn't hate *us*!"

As Caitlin spoke, something strange began to happen.

It happened softly, slowly in the beginning — so softly and slowly that neither of the girls noticed for a minute.

First, the door to their parents' room gently popped open, just a little.

Then, Caitlin's door opened a crack.

Then, Lynne's bedroom door opened slightly, too.

"Hey, Lynne! Look! The bedroom doors are unlocked," Caitlin said.

She felt relieved but confused.

"I don't get it," she said. "Why is the house opening all the doors for us now?"

She paused to think about that. There *had* to be a good explanation. For some reason, the house seemed less menacing, less mean than it had just a few moments before.

But why?

"I think we should run into my room while there's time! The door's open. Let's get my bat right now!" Lynne said. "Then we can try to break through the front door. This place is trying to murder us! I don't care what you say about it. I still *hate this house!*"

Lynne stood at the top of the staircase, near the door to Caitlin's bedroom. Caitlin stood beside her, still thinking.

Caitlin thought very hard. She became so wrapped up in her thoughts that she did not see the danger Lynne suddenly faced.

Just as Lynne got through talking, a huge chunk of plaster broke off the ceiling over her head.

A chunk of heavy plaster, the size of a beach ball, was falling toward Lynne's brains!

By the time Lynne saw it dropping, the chunk was just inches from her head!

She did not even have time to scream.

Caitlin looked up. Her eyes grew wide with shock and fear.

She had absolutely no chance to pull Lynne away from the terrible, crushing weight that was about to smash into her skull!

Chapter Twenty

"I *love* this house!" Caitlin shouted. "I *love it*!"

It was the only thing she could do in time.

It seemed crazy!

It seemed just plain silly, when her sister was about to be bashed by falling plaster!

What good could come from yelling something nice about the old house?

But there was no chance to try anything else. So Caitlin just shouted at the house.

And it worked!

The large chunk of plaster instantly broke apart into dust that floated harmlessly down around Lynne's head and shoulders.

"*Puggggh! Kaaaaph!*" Lynne coughed. "Wha-what happened, Caitlin? You saved my head from being smashed. But how did you do that?"

"Lynne, I think I finally understand something about this house. I understand why this is a haunting house. There is a reason it hates us so much," Caitlin said. "It's such a nice old house, too. It really is when you take a good look at it. It's got beautiful wood on the floors and beautiful shingles on the roof. And everything is built so solid and strong."

"Caitlin, I'm getting worried about you. There you go again about this old house," Lynne said.

"I'm only telling you how much I love this place," Caitlin continued. "Because it has such nice old tile in the bathrooms. And I just love my room! I know you love your room too, don't you?"

Lynne still did not understand what her sister was doing.

"What? Love my room? *No*! I don't, Cait. I *ha* — " Lynne started to say.

"No, you really mean you *love* your room, Lynne!" Caitlin interrupted firmly. "Think about it, *please!* Think about how you really felt before any of this haunting began. I know you loved that room. It's bigger and you didn't have to sleep with me anymore. And you have your own bathroom!"

"Well, yeah. I guess if I think about it like that. It's true," Lynne admitted. "I did like my new room pretty much, I guess. But since then this house has been so terrible to us! And now I really *ha* — "

"No, you mean that you really *love* it just like you did before — *as long as* the house does not try to hurt us anymore," Caitlin interrupted again. "That's what you mean, right? Because I really could be very happy in this house with Dad and Mom. And I know I'll make new friends and I'll like my new school and teachers and everything. Our whole family is going to *love* this place!"

"Caitlin, you really are nuts, I think," Lynne answered. "Sure, I'd like this house fine if it wasn't a haunting house. I'd probably even love it, I guess. But it is a haunting house! Why are you saying all these things?"

"I'm only saying how much I really love this house, Lynne. And how happy we'll all be here — if the house just lets us live peacefully," Caitlin said.

At that moment, all the lights in the house came back on.

And all the locked doors unlocked.

And all the closed shutters snapped open.

The girls could hear things happening all around now.

"But Caitlin, how can such an awful, angry house turn into a good house so fast?" Lynne asked. "Why is it turning the lights on and unlocking the doors and opening the shutters after a whole night of doing horrible things?"

"It's simple, Lynne. The ghost book said there was no way to get rid of the violent forces in a haunting house. But then our bedroom doors opened after I told the house I felt sorry for it," Caitlin explained. "And I remembered how you were always saying you hated the house — right before something bad happened. And so it just made sense that the house was angry because we didn't like it. It was like a person whose feelings were hurt."

"Wow, cool," Lynne said. "Is my big sister smart or what?"

"It was just a lucky guess, Lynne. But when I saw that chunk of plaster break into dust over your head, I knew for sure I was right!" Caitlin said.

"I guess houses sometimes have feelings too,

huh?" Lynne said.

"Yeah, I guess so. We just have to show this house how much we love it. And then I think we'll all really like living here," Caitlin replied.

"It's pretty cool when you think about it. How many kids have a house with feelings?" Lynne said, laughing.

"Not many," Caitlin said. "I *hope!*"

When their parents finally got home, the house was a total mess.

The kitchen was gone. The upstairs ceiling was broken. A living room window was smashed. Their mother's favorite lamp was cracked to bits on the front lawn.

But the girls explained everything that had happened that night — and *why* it had happened. And even though it was hard for their parents to believe the story of a haunting house, they finally did believe it. They had no choice. There was no other logical, scientific explanation.

And they could plainly see the damage.

They made plans to start repairs the next morning — and to turn the old abandoned home into a

116

more beautiful place than it had ever been before.

As Caitlin and Lynne walked upstairs together to get some sleep at last, they looked at each other and smiled.

"Wow, pretty freaky night, huh Cait?" Lynne said. "I'm glad it's over. But you know, I didn't mind it so much. You know why? It's because I — I really *love* this house now!"

"You're such a little kid!" Caitlin said, smiling.

They both laughed and kissed good night.

"Just one thing, though," Lynne said, stopping in the hall. "It's something really important."

"What's that?" Caitlin asked.

"Stay out of the tunnel in my room!" Lynne answered with a chuckle. "My diary is going back in there. Besides, it's way too cool for big sisters!"

They laughed again and went into their bedrooms without fear now.

And the two sisters slept quietly and pleasantly through this night and every other night they ever spent inside their new, old happy and well-loved home.

BE SURE TO READ THESE OTHER COLD, CLAMMY SHIVERS BOOKS.

THE CURSE OF THE NEW KID

LUCAS LYTLE IS USED TO BEING THE NEW KID IN SCHOOL. HE'S TWELVE YEARS OLD — AND HE'S ALREADY BEEN IN EIGHT DIFFERENT SCHOOLS. WHEN EVERYBODY FROM THE SCHOOL BULLIES TO THE CLASS NERDS PICK ON HIM, HE FEELS LIKE HE IS CURSED. BUT THEN STRANGE AND HORRIBLE THINGS START TO HAPPEN TO HIS ENEMIES. AT FIRST LUCAS IS CONFUSED BY WHAT IS HAPPENING. BUT THEN HE STARTS TO ENJOY IT — UNTIL IT BECOMES TOO FRIGHTENING FOR HIM TO HANDLE.

BE SURE TO READ THESE OTHER COLD, CLAMMY SHIVERS BOOKS.

A GHASTLY SHADE OF GREEN

JASON'S MOTHER TAKES HIM AND HIS LITTLE BROTHER ON A VACATION TO FLORIDA – BUT NOT TO THE BEACH. SHE RENTS A LONELY CABIN ON THE EDGE OF THE EVERGLADES, WHERE THE ALLIGATORS BELLOW AND THE PLANTS GROW SO THICK THEY ALMOST BLOT OUT THE LIGHT. JASON DOES NOT LIKE THIS PLACE AT ALL. AND STRANGE THINGS START TO HAPPEN: KEEPSAKES DISAPPEAR FROM HIS DRESSER. HIS BEAGLE WINDS UP MISSING. AT FIRST JASON SUSPECTS BURGLARS, BUT THE TRUTH IS MORE FRIGHTENING. JASON MUST MAKE A DESPERATE EFFORT TO SAVE HIS FAMILY – AND HIMSELF.